Jason's Why

Jason's Why

Beth Goobie

Red Deer Press

Published in Canada by Red Deer Press, 195 Allstate Parkway, Markham, ON, L3R 4T8
Published in the United States by Red Deer Press, 311 Washington Street, Brighton, Massachusetts 02135

www.reddeerpress.com

Edited for the Press by Peter Carver
Cover and text design by Daniel Choi
Cover image courtesy of iStockphoto

We acknowledge with thanks the Canada Council for the Arts, and the Ontario Arts Council for their support of our publishing program. We acknowledge the financial support of the Government of Canada through the Canada Book Fund (CBF) for our publishing activities.

 **Canada Council
for the Arts**   **Conseil des Arts
du Canada**   ONTARIO ARTS COUNCIL
CONSEIL DES ARTS DE L'ONTARIO

Library and Archives Canada Cataloguing in Publication
Goobie, Beth, 1959-
    Jason's why / Beth Goobie.
ISBN 978-0-88995-484-7
    I. Title.
PS8563.O8326J38 2012   jC813'.54   C2012-905181-0

Publisher Cataloging-in-Publication Data (U.S.)
Goobie, Beth.
    Jason's why / Beth Goobie.
[80] p. : col. ill. ; cm.
Summary: A nine-year-old boy sent to a group home by his mother, who can't handle him any longer, learns to trust the people around him, and to talk about his fears despite his concern that his mother might not take him back.
ISBN: 9780889954847 (paper)
1. Group homes -- Juvenile fiction. 2. Interpersonal relations -- Juvenile fiction. 3. Family problems -- Juvenile fiction. I. Title.
[Fic] dc23   PZ7.G6735Ja 2012

Manufactured by Friesens Corporation
Manufactured in Altona, MB, Canada in August 2012
Job#77214

For Val

chapter one

I am at our living-room window. I'm waiting. I can hear my mom. She moves around our house. She goes up and down our stairs. She carries green garbage bags to the door. All my stuff is in those bags. There are three of them.

My name is Jason. I'm nine. Last week, Mom took me to an office. It had a big desk in it. A social-worker lady sat behind the desk. She said, "Hello, Jason." Then she told me her name, but I forgot it. She mostly talked to Mom. I looked out the window, where there was a tree. Birds flew in and out of the tree. Then they flew away.

Mom talks nice to grown-ups. She smiles and uses her nice voice. This makes me nervous, because then she's like someone else. When she's someone else, I

Beth Goobie

don't know what she'll do. I try to be real good when Mom is like this.

The social worker and Mom talked a long time. They talked mostly about me. Mom said I was a problem. She said I yelled and screamed. She said I stole things and ran away. She said I fought with my sister Linda. "I don't know why," Mom said. "Why is Jason like that? Linda doesn't do those things."

The social worker told me something. She said I was going somewhere new to live. It was called a group home. There were other kids my age there. They had problems, too. The staff at the group home would teach me things. They would teach me how to handle my problems. Then I could move back home.

My voice was gone. I wanted to say, "No." I wanted to say, "I'll be good." But my voice just went away. I never knew I could be kicked out of my own house.

Mom looked happy. She smiled at the social worker. The social worker smiled at Mom. Then the social worker smiled at me.

"You'll see, Jason," she said. "The group home will be nice. You'll make new friends there. And you'll get to visit your mom and Linda. You'll call them on the phone."

My voice was still gone. I wanted to say, "I like the

friends I have now. I like my house. I'll be good, I promise." But my voice wouldn't do what I wanted it to do.

Mom and the social worker talked some more. Then Mom and I went home.

So now I'm waiting by our living-room window. Mom drops the last garbage bag beside the front door. "That's all your stuff, Jason," she says. "Now, you listen to me. I don't want you calling and bugging me. You have everything you need inside those bags. Where is that social worker?"

"She's outside," I say. I can see the social worker through the window. She gets out of a blue car and walks toward our house. She looks the same as in her office. She wears the same pure white shirt. I'm sure it never gets dirty.

"No fooling around now, Jason," says Mom. "You behave, you hear me? No screaming."

I know right then it won't help to kick or scream. I think, *Maybe I can hold onto the sofa arm.* Then I know that won't work either. The social worker is here. She'll help Mom pull me off the sofa.

The doorbell rings and Mom opens the door. I can see her—the social worker in her pure white shirt. She's standing on our front porch.

"Hello, Jason," she says. She smiles at me.

I'm scared of her pure white shirt. It's too bright. I stare down at the floor. There's a piece of Lego beside my foot. I pick it up.

"Look, Mom," I say. "Here's part of Linda's Lego. I can take it to her room if you want."

Mom grabs my arm. She takes the Lego. "No, Jason," she says. "You're going now."

She holds my arm so I can't get away. With her other hand, she gets my jacket out of the closet. I want to kick and scream. There are many screams inside me, hurting to come out. But I stand still and let her put on my jacket. Then I bend down to pull on my runners.

Now I smell all the house smells. There's the peanut butter we ate for lunch. There are Mom's cigarettes. I see the color of the sofa. It's brown. I never really looked at it before. I want to go to all the rooms in the house and look at them. What if I never come back?

I have to remember, I think. *When I'm in the group home, I'll my close my eyes and come back.* I put on my runners as slow as I can.

"Hurry up, Jason," says Mom.

I see the hall floor is a real light brown. Slowly, I tie my laces. The social worker's feet are close by. They're wearing purple shoes. I hate purple shoes. I don't want purple shoes in my house. I want to tear them off her feet. I want to throw them out the door and into the street.

I'm scared of those purple shoes. They're here to take me away.

Tears hurt my nose and eyes. They burst out my eyes and run down my face.

"Jason, stop crying," says Mom. She hands me a garbage bag. "Carry this," she says.

The social worker takes a bag. Mom picks up the last one. "Let's go," she says.

The social worker pats my head. I jerk my head away.

Mom opens the door. "Come on, Jason," she says.

I look down the hall. I look at the sofa and TV. I sniff hard to get one last good smell. I want to remember everything.

I pick up the garbage bag. It makes a crinkly noise. The bag is heavy. So are my legs. I walk out the door on my heavy legs. Mom follows me out and closes the door behind us. Now we're out of my house, and it's not my house anymore.

We walk down the sidewalk to the blue car.

Beth Goobie

chapter two

The blue car drives across the city. It drives far from my house. It drives far from my school. It drives far from the park where I play with my friends. The blue car drives past downtown and the day camp I went to last summer. I've never seen any of the streets we're driving through now. I get scared. What will happen to me in a place far away like this?

Finally, the social worker stops the car. She and Mom get my stuff out of the trunk. I sit in the back seat and stare at the closest house. It has a gray roof and a purple front door. *Purple again*, I think. I hate purple front doors.

Mom opens the car door and tells me to get out. I don't want to get out. I don't want to go into the purple-door house. It isn't my house.

"Hurry up, Jason," says Mom.

We walk into the house. Right away, it smells wrong. There's no peanut butter smell. And the floor is yellow, not brown. But there's a TV in the living-room. I like TVs.

The social worker smiles at me. Beside her, I see another lady. "Jason, this is Sue," says the social worker. "Sue works here. She's going to show you the house and your new bedroom."

Mom says, "I have to go. Linda will be home soon."

She hugs me goodbye, but not very much. I hug her tight. I don't want to let go, but she pulls my arms away.

"I have to go, Jason," she says. "You be good now." Mom and the social worker go outside. I watch through the living-room window. They get into the blue car and drive away. Mom doesn't wave goodbye.

"Let's go see your new room, Jason," says Sue.

I'm scared to look at her. There's no one here but her and me. I think, *What if she's a bad lady?* She's a stranger. Mom told me never to talk to strangers. Some strangers are very bad. They kill kids.

"Come on, Jason," Sue says.

I'm skinny and small for my age. But I can run fast. I get ready, in case Sue is going to do something bad. Then, real slow, I look right at her. What I see surprises

Beth Goobie

me. Sue is on her knees. That makes her the same as me—not so big.

"You're scared, aren't you, Jason?" Sue says.

"Yeah," I say. I feel stupid.

Sue has nice eyes. She talks nice and quiet. "Why don't we take your things to your room?" she says. "Then I'll show you the house. You can tell me what you like. And you can tell me what you don't like."

She stands up again. This time, she doesn't look so big. We walk down a hall, past two bedrooms full of boys' stuff. Then we go into another bedroom. Here I see a bed, a dresser, and a toy box. The walls are white. They're pure white. Sue puts my garbage bags beside the bed. Then she shows me the rest of the house.

I'm real careful when we go to the basement. It's dark down there. I stand away from Sue. She looks nice, but you never know. I can see a pool table and a washer and dryer. It looks okay, but then I see some closed doors. I get scared by these closed doors. *What's behind them?* I think. *Anyone could be hiding in there.*

Sue gets out some keys. She unlocks one closed door and shows me a room with canned food and a freezer. The other is just a closet with footballs and soccer balls—that kind of stuff. That makes me feel better. But then I think, *Maybe they lock bad kids in here*. I don't say it out loud.

Sue tells me three other boys live in the group home, too. They're all nine or ten years old. She tells me to go to my room and unpack. Then she says she has to write everything I have on a list. She says I have to show her every single thing.

"Do you remember my name?" she asks.

Of course I do, I think. But I just look down. My voice is gone again.

"My name is Sue," she says. "Can you say that, Jason?"

I'm not sure. "Sue," I say. I sound like a frog. "Sue," I say again, louder.

"That's right," says Sue. She's smiling. "That's good, Jason."

She helps me put my stuff on my new bed. She writes everything I have on a list. She writes down how many socks I have, how many pants and shirts. Then she tells me to put my clothes in the dresser and closet.

I get to pick where things go. I like this. But then Sue puts my model car into the toy box. I don't like her touching my model car. My hands go into fists. If she touches something else, I'm going to hit her. But, for now, I look at the floor.

"Hey, Jason—why don't I let you put your own stuff

Beth Goobie

away?" Sue says. I'm surprised by this. How does Sue know what I'm thinking? She smiles and it makes me smile, too. Then I feel okay.

A door opens at the back of the house. "Hey, Sue!" calls a boy. He sounds happy.

"Hey, Joe!" calls Sue.

A boy comes running to my door. He's native. He hands Sue a notebook. Then he looks at me. I'm not too sure about natives. Mom told me to stay away from them. She said they were trouble. I look at the floor.

Sue reads the notebook. "Your teacher says you had a good day today, Joe," she says.

"Is that what she wrote?" Joe asks. "Awesome!" He grins.

"She wrote that you had a very good day," Sue smiles. "And Joe, this is Jason."

"You the new kid?" Joe asks.

I keep looking at the floor. I don't want to be a new kid.

"Doesn't he know how to talk?" Joe asks.

"Give him time," says Sue. "Remember your first day."

"Okay," says Joe. "Can I go play outside?"

"Change into play clothes first," says Sue.

"Can he come, too?" asks Joe.

"Jason still has some things to unpack," says Sue.

I'm glad she says this. I'm not too sure about playing outside with Joe.

"Do you want some snack, Jason?" asks Sue. "We have snack here every day after school."

"No," I say, even though I'm hungry. I just want everything to go away—Sue, Joe, the group home, everything. Then, just like that, Sue and Joe do go away, and I'm alone in the room. I sit on the bed and look at the walls. They're real white—pure *pure* white. I'm scared I'll get them dirty. Then someone will get mad at me. You never know what can happen when someone gets mad.

I don't let any of my stuff touch the pure white walls.

chapter three

put away all my toys. Then I don't know what to do, so I sit on the bed. Sue comes to the door. I don't like her in the door. There's nowhere to run if things get bad. If I see somewhere to run, I feel better.

"Jason," says Sue, "at 4:30, we have Quiet Time."

I try to listen to her. But my heart pounds real hard because she's standing in the door.

"This is what we do at Quiet Time," Sue says. "The boys go to their rooms for one hour. They do homework."

I look at the floor. I've never done homework before.

"Tomorrow, you go to your new school and meet your new teacher," says Sue. "Today you don't have homework. You can play with your toys."

"Okay," I say, but I just sit on the bed. At home,

Mom sends me to my room when I'm bad. That's what this feels like. I don't know what to do, so I think about Linda. At home, Mom doesn't give us snack like they do here. Sometimes we don't get supper. Linda is only six. She's littler than me. I think maybe she's hungry now.

After a while, Sue comes to the door again. She says, "Everybody has a supper chore to do. Tonight you get to set the table. Come on—I'll show you how."

I've never set a table. I get real worried. I try to listen real good to what Sue says. My heart pounds hard. *What if I break a cup?* I think. Sue looks nice, but you never know. I bang some plates on the table. Not on purpose—by mistake.

"Try to be more careful, Jason," says Sue. That's all. She doesn't yell—nothing like that.

Before supper, all the boys wash their hands. There's Joe, me, and two other boys. One of them is black and one is like me. Sue tells me their names—Dave and Rob. We all sit on the sofa, real quiet, before we go to the table.

Supper tastes good. Sue made it. It's pork chops, potatoes, and corn. I eat lots. I've never seen so much food. When I finish what's on my plate, Sue lets me have more. My tummy hurts, but I eat it. After everyone

Beth Goobie

else leaves the table, Sue lets me eat a third pork chop.

After supper, I clear the table. Then I vacuum under the table. This is hard because my tummy hurts. Joe washes the dishes and Dave dries. Rob has to clean the bathroom.

Joe asks if I can play ball in the back yard. Sue says, "No, not on Jason's first day. He has to stay inside."

I sit on the sofa and watch TV. The other white boy sits beside me.

"Remember my name?" he asks. "It's Rob." He holds up a toy snake and shakes it. "My snake's name is Rob, too," he says. Then he moves the snake near my face. "My snake doesn't like you," Rob says. "See—he wants to bite you."

I think Rob is creepy. I want to punch him, but Sue is in the next room. She'll get mad if I hit Rob, so I don't. I just move my face away.

Joe comes inside and we play cards on the sofa. Rob doesn't want to play cards with us. He doesn't like what's on TV, either. He yells at Sue about this. Then he throws a chair. Sue grabs Rob's arms real quick and puts him onto the floor. Then she sits on him. Rob yells and screams.

My tummy hurts. I run to the bathroom and throw up. I was scared this might happen. *This is where they hurt bad kids*, I think. Sometimes I scream and yell. They'll hurt me, too.

I see Joe standing in the door. "Don't worry," he says. "Haven't you seen a restraint before?"

I wash out my mouth. "What's that?" I ask.

"Sometimes staff restrain us," says Joe. "It doesn't hurt. They just hold you down when you get mad. I used to do that lots—get mad, I mean. I'm getting better now. Staff just hold you down so you can't do anything while you're mad. They don't hit you— nothing like that."

"Oh," I say. Rob is still yelling in the living room. I like what Joe said, but my heart still pounds real hard.

"We have to get into pjs now," says Joe. "After pjs, we get snack."

I get my pjs on. Sue is still sitting on Rob. Rob screams and bangs his feet. Sue asks Joe to get a snack for us.

Joe gets out some bananas. We sit at the kitchen table and eat them. He and Dave tell jokes and laugh. They don't worry about Sue sitting on Rob.

"Now you have to brush your teeth again," says Dave. "You have to brush your teeth all day long around here."

I brush my teeth. In the living room, Rob stops yelling. Now he sits on the sofa and cries. Sue tells me

Rob is on a time-out. He has to sit real quiet and can't talk to us.

Sue asks me to come to the office. The office is behind a locked door beside the kitchen. I get real worried about this.

"Come on in, Jason," Sue says.

I walk into the office. Sue leaves the door open. That makes it feel better. I see a bed, a desk, and a closet. Sue unlocks a cabinet on the wall.

"I have your medicine in here," she says.

I take pills at night and in the morning. A doctor told me if I took the pills, I wouldn't be so bad. They're blue and white.

Sue puts two in a small cup. That's the right number. Sometimes Mom gives me an extra one. She says it makes me sleep better. Then I get dizzy and can't walk good. I count to make sure. I'm glad Sue gives me just two. I take my pills.

I watch some more TV. I sit quiet. I try to be real good. I don't want Sue to sit on me. She's talking to Rob in the office. Everything seems to be all right.

At 8:30, we go to our rooms. Sue says I have fifteen minutes. Then she'll turn out the light. *But I forgot to call home*, I think. I want to talk to Linda. What did she do all day? I'm scared to ask if I can use the phone, but

I call Sue's name. She comes to the door. When I ask, she says I can call home now. But from now on, I have to call home before 8:00.

Mom answers the phone. She sounds mad. I can hear Linda crying close by.

"Stop crying, Linda," says Mom. "I can't hear your brother, you're so loud. What do you want, Jason?"

I don't know what to say. I'm not used to talking to Mom on the phone. It's like talking to my grandma and grandpa in Toronto—way far away.

"How are you?" I ask. "Did you have a nice day?"

"I had a busy day," says Mom. "Very busy."

"Oh," I say. "Can I talk to Linda?"

"No," says Mom. "It's too late. Next time, call earlier. I have to put Linda to bed now. Goodbye."

"Goodbye," I say.

Mom hangs up the phone. I go back to my room.

Sue comes to the door. "How was your call?" she asks.

I say, "Good."

Sue turns out the light. She says she'll close the door after I fall asleep. This is in case there's a fire. Sue says this is the law in group homes. Then she goes back to the office.

I think about sleeping with the door closed. I'm not

Beth Goobie

used to that. It'll be too dark and I'll get scared—even if I'm asleep. Then I get scared Joe might cut off my hair while I'm sleeping. I saw a native do that in a movie. Or Sue might do something bad to me. Or Rob might come into my room with his snake. I think about all these things.

Then I think about Mom. I think I have to be real good to go back home. If I'm real good, maybe Mom will like me.

I'm not too sure about this. I fall asleep.

chapter four

When I wake up, my door is closed. This surprises me because I never close my door. Then I see a strange dresser and closet. And the bedspread is green. How can that be? My bedspread is blue.

This isn't my room, I think. *Where am I?*

Then I see the pure white walls. That makes me remember. *This is the group home*, I think. *Mom and Linda are at my real home. I'm here all alone.*

I'm scared to get up. I think if I get up, Sue will get mad. She'll sit on me.

Someone knocks on the door. Then it opens. A man stands in the door. I've never seen him before. Where is Sue?

"Hello, Jason," he says. "My name is Peter. I'm one of

the staff who work here. It's time to get up now. I want you to get dressed. Then make your bed."

I put on my black pants and blue shirt. I make the bed. Then I sit on it. I think I have to be real careful around this Peter. He's a man, and a man is bigger than a lady. A man can hurt you more.

I have to go to the bathroom, but I don't ask. I think this will make Peter mad. I sit and wait.

Peter comes back. "Are you hungry?" he asks.

"Can I go to the bathroom?" I ask.

Peter says I can use the bathroom whenever I want. Then he makes me a big breakfast—corn flakes, an egg, and some toast. I eat lots. Peter tells me he'll take me to my new school. The other boys have already left for their schools. This is my first day, so I get to go late.

Peter says I have to make a lunch. I've never made a lunch before. Mom made me peanut butter sandwiches for school. So Peter shows me how to get my lunch ready. I make two ham sandwiches. Then I get an apple, a juice box, and some Fruit Wrinkles. *This is a big lunch*, I think. I hide one sandwich in my dresser. This is in case they don't give me supper.

Peter walks me to my new school. It's not far. It's a gray school—like a big gray box. I don't like this school or any school. There are too many kids. There are too many grown-ups. Too many people get me worried. You never know what might happen around all those people.

Peter takes me to meet my new teacher. Her name is Mrs. Pell. Peter says he'll pick me up after school. Then he says goodbye and leaves. Mrs. Pell tells me to sit in a desk at the front of the class. I don't like this because I can't see behind me. There are lots of kids behind me. In my last school, some kids poked me and threw things at my back. I always had to be ready. How can I be ready if I can't see behind me? You have to see behind you to know what's coming.

I sit sideways so I can see behind me. Mrs. Pell doesn't like this. She wants me to sit so I'm looking at her. But I can't—I have to see behind me.

My last teacher did this, too. I got into lots of trouble. I don't want that to happen again. Maybe I can sit the way Mrs. Pell wants and still see behind me. I try sitting with my head turned back.

Mrs. Pell doesn't like this, either. "Turn around, Jason," she says. She sounds mad. But she doesn't have to sit with her back to the class. She can see everyone all the time.

It isn't fair, I think. *I have to see the other kids. You never know.*

Beth Goobie

29

The lunch bell rings real loud. It's so loud, I jerk in my desk. A kid laughs. I think he's laughing at me. That makes me mad.

"Jason," says Mrs. Pell. A boy is standing next to her. "This is Bill. He's going to spend the lunch hour with you. He'll show you around the playground."

"Okay," I say. I get my coat and lunch. Then Bill and I go outside. Right away, I go over to the school wall and sit against it. That way, I can see everybody. But Bill doesn't want to sit by the wall.

"This is stupid," he says. "Let's go sit over there with my friends."

He points to some boys. They're sitting beside the basketball hoop. They look okay, but I want to sit here—where I can see everyone.

"No," I say. "I want to sit here."

"Well, I'm going over there," Bill says. He goes over to his friends and leaves me alone. That's fine with me. Bill is nice, but maybe too nice. Being with someone who's nice won't help me right now. Now, I have to watch out for the kids who aren't nice—the bullies, the bad kids, the ones like me. So I sit by myself and watch while I eat my ham sandwich. I watch while I drink my juice. And I watch while I eat my Fruit Wrinkles—the kind with the funny shapes.

I see some boys from my class—not Bill and his friends, but some others. They're the ones I'm looking for. They're the mean ones. There are always some mean ones. When you're new, you have to find out how strong the mean ones are. You have to make them fight. Then you know how they fight and you can beat them.

The mean boys are playing marbles. I go over to their game and grab a marble. It's the biggest boy's marble. I think he's the meanest.

"Give it back!" says the boy.

I put the marble into my pocket. "Make me!" I say.

I've been in lots of fights. Even if I'm skinny, I know how to kick and hit. I learned this from fighting my dad. He moved away last year, but before that, he hit me lots. So I know how to fight because of him, and I'm good at it. I know I can beat this boy easy. But then two of them jump me.

I've beaten two kids in a fight before. When I fight, I fight real hard. I fight so hard, I can't see anything. There's just a big bubble of mad inside me. I feel that bubble of mad now inside my tummy. It gets bigger and bigger. I think it's going to burst and I'll burst, too. I kick and hit. It feels like the two boys are getting bigger. It feels like there are

Beth Goobie

more and more boys. I fight harder and harder.

Then a teacher stops the fight. The other boys run away and it's just the teacher and me. He's big and I get scared. I kick him to make him move away. He grabs me and puts me down on the ground. Then he sits on me. I get more scared. Inside my head, this teacher turns into my dad. I scream and kick harder.

My dad used to hit me with his belt. It hurt. Sometimes I could hardly walk after. He hit me all the time. Then he and Mom divorced and he moved away. But now it feels like he's come back. I get all mixed up. I think it's my dad sitting on me. I get more and more scared. The other kids have all gone into the school. Everything is quiet, except for my screaming. No one will see if this man hurts me.

The teacher holds my arms. He doesn't hit me. He just holds me tight so I can't move. Slowly, the bubble of mad inside me goes away. Now I can see the teacher isn't my dad.

"Let me go!" I say.

"I'm Mr. Warner," says the man. "I'm your school principal. I'm going to let you up now. I want you to stand quietly."

He lets me up slow. I want to run, but he keeps a hand on my arm.

"Come inside," he says. "We need to talk."

Mr. Warner takes me to his office. He says he wants me to talk to the other boys. He wants me to say I'm sorry. He wants me to give back the marble.

Mr. Warner calls the other boys into his office. I look at the meanest boy. His name is Larry. I don't care about the marble. I think Larry knows this. He knows you have to watch out for the big kids. Whoever is bigger will get you. That's the way it is.

Now I know a little about how Larry fights. Tomorrow, I'll fight him again to find out more. Then I'll know everything. If Larry knows I'm stronger, he'll be scared of me. Then he'll leave me alone.

I give back Larry's marble. I say I'm sorry. Larry and I shake hands.

Then we go back to class. I have to sit at the front again. Mrs. Pell keeps saying, "Turn around, Jason." She doesn't know I have to see behind me.

I try to think about the math she's teaching. I try to think about three times six, and seventy divided by seven. But I keep thinking about the kids behind me. And I think about Linda. I bet she just got peanut butter sandwiches for lunch today. It makes me feel bad about eating my ham sandwich.

Mrs. Pell asks why I haven't done my work. I'm busy

Beth Goobie

thinking about Linda, and it's loud inside my head. So when Mrs. Pell talks to me, the big bubble of mad comes back. I yell at Mrs. Pell. I throw my math book on the floor.

Mrs. Pell sends me to Mr. Warner's office. I wait there until Sue comes to pick me up. Mr. Warner says I can't come back until tomorrow. I'm suspended for today.

That's fine with me. I don't want to go to that school. There are too many kids. You can't watch them all. Besides, it's not my school. I want my school back.

chapter five

walk beside Sue. I watch her real close. When I can, I'm going to run. When you get kicked out of school, grown-ups hit you. They hit and yell.

Sue looks like she can run fast. She walks close beside me. She asks me what happened. I tell her the boys beat me up.

Sue says, "Mr. Warner saw what happened, Jason. He says you started it."

I say, "No, I didn't."

I think, *How can I run away when she's this close?*

I can see the group home down the street. We're getting close. Sue walks beside me all the way to the back door. There's a rule about this in the group home. The boys can only go in the back door. I think this is real stupid. In my house, I can go in any door I want.

Beth Goobie

But I'm in a house that isn't my house.

Staff mostly use the front door. I think Sue walks me to the back door because she knows I want to run. We go inside and I take off my shoes like I'm supposed to.

Sue says, "Come into the office, Jason."

We go past the kitchen, into the office. Peter is sitting at the desk. I think, *There are two of them. They'll hurt me real bad.*

Sue says, "You can sit on the bed, Jason."

I sit on the staff bed. At night, the staff sleep like the boys do. Maybe I'll run away sometime when they're asleep.

I watch their hands and feet. When hands and feet move fast, you're going to get hit. Peter watches me from the desk. Sue stands in the door. I hate her standing in the door. I get my hands and feet ready to fight.

Then I think, *Why is it so quiet?*

Peter's hands and feet aren't moving. They aren't getting ready to fight. Neither are Sue's—she has her hands in her pockets. I'm not too sure about this. My mom yells when I do something wrong. She hits me with whatever is around.

I look at their faces. Peter is smiling a little. Then I look at Sue. She's still standing in the door.

Peter says, "Jason, does it make you nervous that Sue is standing in the door?"

I'm surprised by this. How does he know what I'm thinking? "Yes," I say, real low. I don't want to make Sue mad.

"We don't want you to feel nervous," says Peter. "We need to talk to you, but we want you to feel good about it. Where would you like Sue to be?"

I think this is weird, but nice. "Maybe over there," I say. I point to the corner beside the desk.

"That's okay with me," says Sue. She walks to the corner and stands there. I get more surprised when she does this. And the door feels better now.

Peter starts to talk. He talks low and quiet. He talks slow. I get a bit worried, but not too bad. Peter says, "Mr. Warner says you took a boy's marble. Then you hit the boy. That started a fight."

I don't say anything. I think if I say nothing, that'll be best.

"That's what happened, isn't it?" says Peter.

"It's not my school," I say real quiet. Inside me, I feel a bubble of mad start to grow.

"It's hard to move to a new school, isn't it, Jason?" says Peter.

"I want my school," I say. "I want my house. I want

Beth Goobie

my mom and sister. I don't want here. I hate this place!"

Then I stop talking. I think maybe I said too much. They'll tell Mom. Then she'll get mad and not let me come home—not ever.

"Tomorrow, you'll go back to your new school," says Peter. "But this time, Ann will be there. She'll be there just for you. She'll help you with your school work."

I don't know about this Ann. "I don't want to go to that school," I say.

Peter and Sue don't say anything.

"I want to go to my room," I say.

"Okay, Jason," says Peter. "You can go. But I want you to leave your door open."

Then I can't climb out the window, I think. Now I get real sad. I know they'll watch me good. I can't run away. I can't run home. I can't see Linda and talk to her.

I go to my room. *Why didn't Peter yell or hit me?* I think. But maybe he still will. If he does, I'll be ready for him. I sit down on the bed and wait.

chapter six

Peter brings me some math. He says I have to do homework until school lets out. I think, *That isn't work from my school. I won't do it.*

I sit on the bed. I look at the pure white walls. I think, *Get me out of here! Get me out!* The words shout inside my head. I want to go home, but I don't know how to get there. Where is my house from here?

Joe comes home from school. Peter tells him to change into his play clothes. Joe goes into his room and changes. I think, *Why is he doing what they say? They aren't his mom or dad.*

Peter tells me I can come out of my room now. Joe and I go to the living room and play cards.

"You get kicked out of school?" Joe asks.

"Yeah," I say. "I don't care. It's a stupid school."

Beth Goobie

39

Joe says, "I used to get kicked out of school a lot. I still do, sometimes. But that's dumb, you know. Because you fail your year." Then he says, "The staff here are okay. Sometimes they say dumb things. I think some of the rules are stupid. I don't want to be here forever. I want to go live with a family."

"Don't you have one?" I ask.

"Not a good one," he says. "They hurt me. I want a real mom and dad—ones that care. That would be awesome." Then Joe says another thing. "They don't beat you up here."

"I saw what happened to Rob last night," I say. "And the principal did that to me this afternoon."

"He put you in a restraint?" says Joe.

"Yeah—if that's what you call it," I say.

"Okay, but did he hit you?" asks Joe.

"He grabbed me and put me on the ground," I say.

"What were you doing?" asks Joe.

I don't say anything. I don't want to talk about that.

"Did he hurt you?" asks Joe.

"My arms hurt after," I say.

"Yeah," says Joe. "They say they won't hurt you, but sometimes they do—a little. But it isn't the same as getting beat up. Staff don't mean to hurt you. They're just stopping you, that's all."

"Maybe," I say. I'm not too sure about this.

We play more cards. Rob and Dave come home from school. We all wash our hands. Then we have to sit quiet on the sofa again. This is to show we're ready to have snack. I think this is stupid, but I sit like the other boys. Then we all have apple juice and some trail mix—peanuts, raisins, and Smarties. Yummy!

Peter tells me it's Quiet Time. That means I have to go to my room. When I'm in my room, Peter brings me some more math. I don't want to do math. I never had to do math at my house. I'm not used to all this work. I'm not used to all these rules. There are too many staff at this group home. There are too many boys. I think, *Get me out of here! Get me out!*

The bubble of mad is inside me again. I pick up the math book Peter gave me. I throw it at the pure white walls. "I don't want to do this work!" I say, real loud.

I feel the mad bubble start to grow. "No!" I yell. Inside me, the mad bubble grows and grows. "No!" I yell again.

I pick up something else and throw it. I don't even know what it is. I pick up another thing and throw it, too.

Peter runs into the room. He grabs my arms. I think he's going to throw me against the wall like my dad used to do. So I kick him. Peter lifts me into the air and I scream. Then he puts me down onto the bed. My face is pushed into the pillow and I can't breathe. Peter puts my arms behind my back. Then he sits on me.

I turn my face to breathe. I yell, "Get off me!" I scream and kick. The mad bubble gets bigger and bigger. It gets so big, it blows up.

I scream when it blows up. All of the madness comes out of me. Then it goes away. After it's gone, I lie on the bed and cry. Peter says, "It's okay, Jason. Just cry. It's okay to cry."

I keep crying. I'm so scared. I don't know what's going on. I don't know what will happen to me here. And there's a big man sitting on me. It makes me think of my dad and how he hurt me.

Peter says, "It's okay, Jason." But it isn't okay. Nothing is okay. I'm so tired from all this crying.

Peter lets go of my arms. He stands up. I don't move. My arms are sore. My eyes hurt from crying. The bed is wet under my face. I'm tired.

I fall asleep.

chapter seven

wake up from a bad dream. My dad was in the dream. For a second, I think he's here with me in my bedroom now. Then I know he isn't. I'm alone.

I look around me. I'm in a dark room, but the door is open. Then I see my bedspread is green. I remember I'm in the group home.

Why did Mom do this to me? I think. *Why did she put me here?*

Peter walks by the door. He sees I'm awake. He says, "Can I come in, Jason?"

I want to say no. "Yes," I say. It's their house.

He sits on the floor. This makes me feel better because now he's not so big. And because he won't be able to hit me as fast. Still, I get ready, just in case.

"You slept a long time," Peter says. "Are you hungry?"

I'm real hungry. "Yes," I say.

"I'm going to bring you some supper," Peter says. "After you eat, we'll talk."

I don't want to talk. I think, *What will we talk about?* I'm not used to all this talking.

Peter brings me supper. There's a lot. I want to save some to put into my dresser with the ham sandwich. But Peter watches me eat, so I can't.

My tummy feels very full when I'm done. Peter takes the empty plate from me. Then he sits on the floor again. I sit on the bed. The door is open, so there's somewhere to run.

Peter says, "Do you know why I held you down on your bed?"

Right away, I don't like this talking. It makes me feel scared. I think maybe he's going to do it again. I don't say anything.

Peter says, "Jason, I'm not going to hurt you."

"You hurt me already," I say.

"That's called a restraint," says Peter. "In this house, you may not throw things. You may not break things. We'll restrain you if you try to hurt someone. Or if you try to hurt yourself. Do you know what a restraint is?"

"Yes," I say. "That's when they grab you and throw you down. They hold you so tight, your arms hurt."

"I'm sorry if I hurt you," says Peter. "But you kicked me. I held you still so you couldn't hurt me or yourself. Sometimes you get so angry, you can't think. Then you do things you wouldn't normally do. I held you until you weren't angry anymore."

"I'm still mad," I say.

"What are you mad about?" asks Peter.

"You," I say. "I don't want to be here. I want to go home."

Peter says, "That's not up to me. Your mother asked us to take care of you for a while. You need to work out some problems here."

This makes me scared. I think, *Mom wants to get rid of me. How come nobody asks me what I want?* But I don't say it.

"What are you thinking about, Jason?" asks Peter.

I don't think I'll tell him. He's a grown-up and will tell Mom. Then she'll get mad and not let me come home. "Nothing," I say.

"This house isn't like your house," says Peter. "We have different rules here. You have to follow them like everyone else. I know things feel new and different. You don't have to be perfect. We'll give you chances to remember the rules. But you may not hurt yourself or anyone else. And no one here will hurt you."

Beth Goobie

I think about Rob and his snake, but I don't say anything about it. "I want to call my sister," I say.

"Sure," says Peter.

I look at the floor. I'm not too sure about asking this. "Can you call for me?" I say real quick. "Last night I called and my mom didn't let me talk to her."

Peter looks at me real close. "Why was that, Jason?" he asks.

I can't stop it. The words burst out of me. "She said it was too late, but Linda was right there," I say. "I could hear her crying. What if Linda didn't get supper? Maybe she fell and hurt herself. I want to talk to her and know if she's all right."

"Why do you think Linda might not get supper?" asks Peter.

"Sometimes Mom doesn't give us supper," I say. "When we're bad. I'm bad a lot. Linda, not so much." I stop for a second. I'm thinking about how mad Mom will get if she hears I said that. But there are too many words inside me. They're busting to get out.

"See—my mom yells," I tell Peter. "Sometimes, she hits. Not so much with Linda because Linda's mostly good. Mom's nicer with her. But with me, well—she gets mad a lot. Once, she hurt my arm. She pushed me down the stairs and I fell on it. My arm got real big and dark. Mom told the doctor it got stuck in a door, but it didn't.

"When Mom gets mad, I mostly go away—away from the house. I run outside before she can get me. I ride around on my bike or go to the park. Sometimes, I visit my friend Benny. I stay away until it gets dark. Then Mom's okay again. When I come home, she doesn't say anything."

I talk more and more. I can't stop. I forget I'm talking to Peter. I forget Mom will be mad. I tell about the time she locked me outside at night. Then I had to sleep on the porch without a jacket. I tell about other things, too. The words come out and out. They've been inside a long time. They're like the bubble of mad, bursting free.

But I don't tell Peter about one thing—my dad and what he did to me. I don't even want to think about it. That secret is too big to tell—for now.

Finally, I stop talking. Peter tells me he's glad I told him what I did. Then he calls my mom. After that, I get to talk to Linda.

"What are you doing?" I ask her.

"Watching my Care Bears DVD," she says. "When are you coming home?"

"I don't know," I say. "I want to come home now."

"Yeah," says Linda. "Come home now. This house is poopy without you."

She laughs and I laugh, too. Then Mom comes onto the phone. She says Linda has to go to bed.

"Goodnight, Jason," she says. "You be good, now."

"Goodnight," I say.

When I hang up the phone, I feel better. Linda sounded good, and I'm real glad about that. I get into bed and think about this. While I'm thinking about it, Sue comes into my room.

"Here, Jason," she says. "This teddy bear is for you. It's yours to keep."

Then she goes out again. I look at the bear a long time after lights out. It's soft and brown and very nice, but it's from here. I don't want to be here. Here is too different, with too many new things. At home, I know the way everything is. At home is where I'm me. Here, I'm not-me. I don't know who I am.

I want Linda, and my house, and to be good for Mom. *No, not good*, I think. *Perfect. I want to be perfect for Mom. If I'm perfect, then Mom will let me come home again.*

Tomorrow, I think. *Tomorrow I'm going to be perfect for Mom.*

I fall asleep.

chapter eight

wake up in the morning. Right away, I see I'm not home again. All I have is the teddy bear, the green bedspread, and the pure white walls. Someone knocks on my door. Then the door opens and a lady sticks in her head. I've never seen this lady before.

"Good morning, Jason," she says. "My name is Rose. It's time to get up for breakfast."

I get worried. Who is this Rose? Is she like Peter and Sue? Did she hear about the restraint? Did it make her mad?

I feel real stupid about the restraint. Peter is nice. I wish I didn't kick him. The other boys must think I'm dumb. I think maybe I won't get up.

Someone knocks on my door again. Rose says, "Are you up, Jason?"

I say, "Yeah." I get up real slow. I put on my black pants and blue shirt.

Rose knocks on my door and opens it. "Good!" she says. "You're up! Now you need to make your bed. And clean up your room. When it's good and clean, I'll check it. Then you can have breakfast."

I think that's a lot to do before breakfast. I'm real hungry. I put all my junk under the bed. But Rose looks there right away. She makes me put everything into my toy box and dresser.

Then I have to wash my hands. I have to sit on the sofa good and straight before I can eat. The other boys are all sitting there, too.

At breakfast, Joe talks to Rose. Rob and Dave joke with each other. I look at the table and eat. I'm surprised— no one tells me that I'm dumb because of the restraint. They act like it never even happened.

After breakfast, Joe rides a bike to his school. Rob and Dave take a school bus to theirs. Rose walks me to my school. I ask her, "Where are Sue and Peter?"

She says, "They don't work today."

I say, "How many staff work at this house?"

She says, "Three—Sue, Peter, and me. Sometimes you'll meet other staff, but not very often. Sue, Peter, and I are there all the time."

I think, *Not all the time.* Now I finally know them a bit, Sue and Peter are gone. I want to go home, where it's only Linda, Mom, and me.

Rose and I get to my new school. But we don't go to my class. We go to the principal's office. Mr. Warner is sitting at his desk. He tells me again how bad it is to fight. Then he goes to the door and calls in a lady. She smiles at me.

"Jason, this is Ann," says Mr. Warner. "She's here just for you. She'll help you do your work and catch up with the rest of the class."

I don't like this. The other kids will think I'm weird. They'll think I can't do the work on my own. They'll say I'm dumb, and they'll be right. I am dumb. That's why my mom hates me. That's why she wants to get rid of me.

Ann says, "Hello, Jason." I don't say anything.

Ann and I walk to my class. I get real mad inside when she puts her chair beside my desk. The other kids stare. But then Mrs. Pell says I can move to the back of the class. She says it'll be easier for everyone to see the board. Ann is real big—bigger than most ladies. I don't think anyone could see around her.

So now I get a desk at the back of the room. I'm real

Beth Goobie

glad about this. Finally, I can see what the other kids are doing.

Ann talks quiet and slow. I like this. When she talks, I think maybe I can get the math right. Maybe I can even get it right on a test. I'll get the test perfect! Then I'll show the perfect test to my mom. And maybe then she'll let me come home.

chapter nine

Ann stands close by and spies on me at recess. I think she's my recess cop. She's spying on me so I won't fight. But she doesn't need to worry. I just sit against the wall and watch everyone. Bill asks me to play with his friends, but I say no. For now, I'm just watching.

At lunch, Rose comes to the school. She says I have to go to a meeting. She says this is a meeting with Mom and Debbie, my social worker. We drive to Debbie's office. Linda is in the waiting room. Rose gets out some toys for us to play with. Then she goes into the meeting.

"Play Barrel of Monkeys with me," Linda says.

I try, but it's hard for me to think about playing. The office door is closed, but I can hear the grown-ups talking behind it. I can tell Mom is mad—her voice is

Beth Goobie

real loud. I'm not too sure about this. I think maybe they told Mom the things I told Peter. Now Mom is mad and she'll never let me come home.

Finally, Rose lets Linda and me come into the office. Like I thought, Mom looks real mad. I sit far away from her. Linda sits beside me. I look at the floor. Now I know for sure they told Mom what I said about her.

Debbie is wearing her pure white shirt. She says, "Jason, your mom and I have had a talk."

I think, *Yeah, I know. I heard you shouting.* But I don't say it.

Debbie says more. "Your mom and I have decided something. For now, she's going to visit you at the group home. Later, we can talk about visits at your house."

I think, *I can't go home. That's what she means. I can never go home.*

I look at Mom. She says, "You lied about me, Jason. Because you lied, I have to visit you at the group home. That way, the staff will see I don't hit you."

I get real scared at this. I look away from Mom. I look away from Rose. I don't look at Debbie, either. I think, *They don't believe me. They believe Mom. She talks real good to grown-ups.*

I want to say, "No." But I get scared and my voice is gone.

Linda moves closer to me. She takes my hand. Everything gets real quiet.

Debbie says, "Jason, your mom says you're not telling the truth. I don't want you to think we don't believe you. The staff don't know you very well. We don't know your mom, either. But we want to keep you safe."

I'm not too sure what this means. I can feel Mom getting madder.

Rose says, "Do you understand what we're saying, Jason?"

I don't say anything.

"Jason, can you look at me?" asks Rose.

I try real hard. But my eyes get stuck to the floor.

Rose says, "Lots of times, two people will say different things about something that happened. You say your mother hurt you. Your mother says she didn't. We don't know what happened, but we want to keep you safe. So we want to be with you when you visit your mother."

Now Mom gets real mad. She says, "I don't like being called a liar. I can't come to the group home every other day. I have to go to work. I have to take care of Linda. And I don't have a car to drive there."

I think, *Mom won't visit me. I won't see Linda ever again.*

Linda holds my hand tighter.

"We'll do the driving," says Rose. "We'll pick up you and Linda. Then we'll drive you home again."

"I don't like the whole idea," says Mom. "You're telling me I can't be trusted with my own kid. I put Jason in the group home because he has a problem. Now you're blaming me. Jason is the problem."

I don't listen anymore. Rose and Debbie talk to Mom. Linda and I sit real quiet. I look at the floor.

But something works right. At the end of the meeting, Mom says she'll visit on Saturday. And she'll bring Linda with her.

I think Rose and Debbie are real smart. I think, *How did they get Mom to stop being mad?*

Then I think, *But maybe Mom will change her mind again. Maybe she won't come to visit on Saturday.*

But maybe she will. You never know.

chapter ten

R ose drives me back to the group home. She says, "How do you feel about the meeting, Jason?"

I say, "I didn't want you to tell my mom what I said."

Rose says, "Our job is to keep you safe. You told us your mom hurt you. That means we have to make sure it doesn't happen again. It's against the law for adults to hurt children. It's wrong."

"But I want to go home," I say. "If Mom is mad, she won't let me."

Rose doesn't say anything about this. When we get to the group home, the other boys are there. Sue is working, too. She tells me to change into my play clothes. Then I wash my hands. I sit real quiet on the sofa with the other boys. I think I'm getting used to the rules. Then I get to eat snack. It's chocolate pudding—yummy!

Joe says, "Can I play the piano?"

I think, *Where's the piano?* Then I see it's in the living room. I guess I've been so worried, I didn't really look at it before. Joe sits down on the piano bench and plays a cool song. It's called "The Pink Panther." He plays it again. I watch real close.

Rose says, "Can you play the piano, Jason?"

I say, "No." I've never played a piano. I know I could never do anything like that.

Joe says, "I never knew how before I came here to live. Rose taught me. You can do it if I can. See, it goes like this. Pretty awesome, eh?"

He plays "The Pink Panther" again. I stand beside him and watch. I think I've changed my mind about Joe and natives. I think my mom is wrong about them. Joe is cool. He treats me nice. But he plays too fast. I can't see what he's doing.

Rose says, "Joe, let Jason sit down on the bench."

She pulls up a chair. Joe gets off the bench and I sit down. I'm not too sure about this. The piano looks real big. And I'm dumb and stupid. I know this if I know anything. So I know I won't be able to play the piano. Then Rose won't like me anymore. Or Joe.

Rose says, "Jason, before we start, I want you to know something. This is the most important thing I'll ever tell you about the piano."

I get real nervous. What is this most important thing? I'll get it wrong—I know I will. I always do.

Rose says, "Are you listening?"

I don't say anything. I want to get up off the piano bench. I want to go to my room. I never want to see a piano again. Or Rose.

Rose says, "Now I'm going to tell you what it is. This is the most important thing for you to know about the piano. I want you to make sure you make lots and LOTS of mistakes."

It gets real quiet. I stare at the piano. I can't believe what Rose said. *She wants me to make mistakes?* I think. *I'm real good at mistakes.*

I let out a big breath. I look at Rose. She smiles at me. Joe laughs.

"I can do that," I say.

"Me, too!" says Joe. "I'm real awesome at mistakes."

"Okay," says Rose. "Put your hands on the piano, Jason. Push down your fingers. See how it sounds."

I'm still nervous, but I put my hands on the piano. Then I push down a finger. This makes a loud sound come out of the piano. I pull my hand away and Joe laughs again.

"Now, Joe," says Rose. "Shh. That was good, Jason. Try it again."

I look at Joe. He grins at me. I grin back. *This is okay*, I think. I push down another finger. The piano makes a different sound.

"Good!" says Rose. She moves my hand around the piano. She shows me how to make high sounds and low sounds. She shows me how to play sounds that are close together. Then she shows me how to play sounds that are far apart. She says a sound is called a "note." A piano has a LOT of notes.

"That was very good, Jason," says Rose. "I think that's enough for your first lesson."

"Yeah," says Joe. He's setting the table for supper. "You have awesome fingers. I'm going to call you the Finger Man!"

We laugh about this. Then I go to my room for Quiet Time. Sue brings me some math to do. I open the book but it's hard to think about math. I'm too busy thinking about notes. There are so many of them. You can play them loud or soft. You can play them fast or slow. And I didn't do anything wrong! No one yelled at me. I go to my bedroom door and look out at the piano. *Finger Man*, I think. *That's almost as good as*

Superman. Someday, I'm going to play "The Pink Panther" like Joe.

After supper, I call home. Mom sounds mad, but she lets me talk to Linda. I tell Linda to listen. Then I play some notes on the piano for her. "That's a piano," I tell her. "It's full of notes—hundreds of them."

"Oh," she says. "It sounds like being happy."

"It is happy!" I say. "When you visit on Saturday, I'll show you some more happy notes."

Then I say goodbye and hang up the phone. When I go to bed, I think about living in this place. It's so different from my home. The staff aren't like my mom. I like them a lot, and I wonder if that's wrong. Because you're supposed to love your mom best—no matter what.

But the staff don't yell, I think. *They don't hit. They feed me lots. And they like mistakes.*

I think about this for a long time. I'm not too sure about any of it. But I know one thing for sure—I'm going to play that piano again.

I fall asleep.

chapter eleven

The next day, Rose walks me to school. Then she goes back to the group home. I stand beside the wall and watch the other kids play. I can see Bill playing marbles with some of his friends. Larry isn't one of them. I think today I'd like to play with Bill and his friends. But I don't have a marble.

Then I remember the gum ball Joe gave me at breakfast. It's kind of like a marble. I go over to Bill and ask if I can play. I show him the gum ball and say it'll be my marble. Bill and his friends laugh. They say I can play.

I line up a shot with my gum ball. I think I can take out a blue marble real easy. But then someone pushes me from behind. I fall over and he grabs my gum ball. It's Larry. He grins and laughs at me. Then he pops my gum ball into his mouth and chews it.

"Come on, loser!" he says. "A gum ball for a marble! What's wrong with you, group-home boy? Did you lose all your marbles?"

I'm madder than mad. That gum ball was from Joe. It made me a friend of his. And it was making me friends here, too. I get to my feet real slow. All around me, kids are shouting, "Fight! Fight!" I can see it in their faces—they want a fight. If I fight Larry, they'll like me. Kids always like the biggest, meanest guy. That was the way it was in my last school. That's the way it is in all schools.

My heart is real loud. I can't think. I get my hands and feet ready. If everyone wants a fight, I'll give them one.

Then Mr. Warner butts in. He runs over and stands between Larry and me. "What's going on?" he asks.

"It's a fight," says a girl. "They were going to fight."

The kids look disappointed. They wanted a fight and now they won't get one. They start to walk away.

"What was the fight about?" asks Mr. Warner.

Bill steps forward. He looks upset, but not at me. "Larry started the fight," he says. "Jason was playing marbles with us. Everything was okay. Then Larry came over. He pushed Jason and grabbed his gum ball."

"His gum ball?" Mr. Warner asks. He looks mixed-up.

"He didn't have a marble," Bill says. "So he used a gum ball."

Some of the kids start to laugh. I get embarrassed. Then a boy I don't know punches my arm—not hard, but as if he likes me. And I see the kids think my gum ball is funny, not stupid. I laugh, too.

"I didn't take no gum ball!" Larry says. "Try and prove it." He swallows my chewed-up gum ball—I see it go down his throat. "See?" Larry says. He opens his mouth and sticks out his tongue. "No gum," he says.

"Larry took Jason's gum ball," Bill says. He sounds mad. "I saw it happen."

Mr. Warner looks at me. "Well, Jason," he says. "What do you have to say about this?"

I think real fast. I know Larry is just paying me back for our last fight. Then I look at the kids who are standing around. I see some who don't want me to fight—Bill and his friends, but some others, too. I'm surprised by this. *I don't have to fight to make them like me*, I think. *They like me because they think I'm funny.*

So I say, "I don't care about the gum ball. I didn't want to eat it anyway. My dog sat on it this morning before I came to school."

All the kids start to laugh. They laugh real hard. Even Mr. Warner laughs. The only person who isn't laughing is Larry. He looks sick.

The bell rings and the kids go into the school. Mr. Warner puts his hand on my shoulder. "Good for you, Jason!" he says. "You did very well. You stayed out of a fight. And you made some new friends."

I don't know what to say. A principal has never said anything like that to me before. "A dog didn't really sit on my gum ball," I tell him. "I made that up. I don't even have a dog."

Mr. Warner grins. "I won't tell Larry if you won't," he says.

I grin back. "Okay," I say. "I promise I won't."

"Now, off to class," says Mr. Warner, and I run into the school.

Beth Goobie

chapter twelve

Then comes the day I've been waiting for. It's Saturday, and Mom and Linda are coming to visit. All morning, I do chores. When I clean my room, I find the ham sandwich I hid in my dresser. I forgot I put it there. It smells bad so I throw it out. I'm pretty sure now they'll give me all my suppers.

When I finish cleaning my room, I have to vacuum the living room. Then I dust. I feel like Cinderella, but finally I'm done.

We have lunch. Then there's nothing to do but wait. Mom and Linda are supposed to get here at 1:30. That feels like hours away. Joe wants me to play outside, but I'm too nervous. My heart is loud and my tummy hurts. *How will Mom be when she gets here?* I think. I sit on the sofa and watch out the window. *Will she be mad? Will she be tired? Will she just want to go home again?*

A car pulls up outside the house. Mom is in the front seat beside Peter. Linda is in the back. I start to run out the front door, but Sue tells me to wait. So I kneel on the sofa and wave out the window. Linda waves back. Mom does, too—sort of.

They come in the front door. Mom says, "Hi, Jason." She doesn't smile. Linda gives me a big smile, but she looks nervous. Sue tells me to show them around the house. I show them my room, then the rest of the house. It's bigger than our house. Linda holds tight onto my hand. Mom is real quiet.

I bring some toys to the living room so Linda can play. Mom sits on the sofa and watches. Sue is in the kitchen, baking cookies. Peter and Joe are playing pool in the basement.

"I did good this week," I tell Mom.

"You got into a fight," she says.

"Only on the first day," I say. "Not since then."

She doesn't say anything.

"I made some new friends," I say. "At school and here."

Mom looks at her watch. Already she's thinking about going home. *She wants to go home and leave me*

Beth Goobie

here, I think. *Forever. She wants to leave me here forever.*

"I learned to play the piano," I say. "Look, Linda—now I can show you the happy notes."

My heart is loud and my head hurts. All I can think is, *Make Mom talk! Make Mom listen! Make Mom want to be here!*

I go to the piano. I sit on the bench. Linda comes over and stands beside me. I think of the song Rose is teaching me—"Mary Had A Little Lamb." But it's not good enough. It doesn't play high and low. I need something big. I need something loud. I need something that will talk to Mom and tell her what I want.

I put a finger on the piano and push down a note. I play another note. Then I just let my fingers do what they want. They go high and low. They play all over the piano. They play loud. They play soft. Linda is smiling. But when I look at Mom, she isn't looking at me. She's looking at the floor.

Look at me! I think. *I want you to look at me!*

But Mom doesn't. She just looks at the floor. I get so sad then—sad and mad. I'm trying so hard, but I can't make Mom look at me. *She doesn't love me,* I think. *She'll never love me.*

My arms come up and I smash them hard onto

the piano. I smash again and again. Now the piano is talking to my mom. It's talking loud and it's talking mad. *Bang!* I think. *Bang! Crash! Bang!*

Peter runs into the living room. He grabs my arms and pulls them off the piano. Then he and Sue lift me onto the floor and sit on me. This makes me madder and I start to fight. But they're stronger than me and they hold me down.

I start to cry. It all bursts out of me. "Mom hates me!" I say. "I want her to love me, but she doesn't. No matter what I do, she won't love me. How can I make her love me? How?"

Peter and Sue let me up. I sit with my hands over my face. Now I'm scared. Mom heard what I said. For sure, she'll really hate me.

It gets real quiet. I can't look. I can't look at anyone.

Linda sits down beside me. "I love you, Jason," she says. "Love you lots." She puts a hand on my arm and pats it. I cry harder.

Finally, Mom says something. She says, "I don't hate you, Jason. We've had some hard times, it's true. But I do love you. And I'm doing my best." She sits real quiet for a bit. Then she looks at me and I see it in her eyes. She's scared like I'm scared. She doesn't know what to do, either.

Beth Goobie

"I want to be good, Mom," I say. "I want to be perfect for you."

Now Mom starts to cry, too. "Come here, Jason," she says.

My heart gets real loud. I get up slow and walk over to her.

"Oh, Jason," she says, and then she hugs me—tight and close, like she hugs Linda. "My boy," Mom says. "I don't know what to do with you. I don't know how to help you. You have problems and you need help. I'm not saying you can never move home again. But you need to be in this group home for now."

Mom stops and thinks a bit. She's still crying. "And maybe I need help, too," she says. "I'm not perfect, either. Maybe I've made mistakes, too."

"It's okay, Mom," I say. "Just cry. It's okay to cry, you know. It makes you tired, but it's okay."

Mom smiles a little. Then Linda butts in and we have to hug her, too. All three of us hug tight, and I feel it—something is different. I still have to live in the group home, but now I know it won't be forever. And Mom is going to try to be good, just like me. My heart stops pounding so loud, and my head doesn't hurt so much. I take a big breath. Peter gives me some Kleenex and I blow my nose.

Sue brings out some juice and cookies. After we eat the cookies, Mom goes to the office and talks to Sue. Then she and Linda have to go. At the front door, Mom pats my face. She says, "The staff say you're doing well, Jason. We'll come visit again next Saturday."

She smiles and it's a real smile. I can tell she means it just for me.

Linda's smile is real, too. "Bye bye, Jason," she says. "Play more happy notes when you call me tonight."

I watch from the window as Mom and Linda walk to the car. Linda gets into the back and Mom gets into the front. Sue honks the horn as they drive away.

Then they're gone again. I stare out at the street. How can that be—my mom and sister were here, and now they're just gone away.

But next Saturday, I think. *They'll be here again. It's not forever.*

But still it's hard. I don't know what's going to happen. *Mom said she loved me*, I think. *But will she really let me move home again? Or will I be stuck in this group home maybe forever?*

All these questions, and I don't know the answers. If only I did—right now. *But I guess I can't,* I think. *I can't make the answers happen right now. I'll have to wait.*

Joe comes into the living room. "Hey, Jason," he says. "Want to play cards?"

And you know, I think, *maybe this place isn't so bad.*

"Okay," I say, and Joe gets out the cards.

Acknowledgments

The author would like to thank Harold Glass, MSW, RSW, for his valuable and valued comments concerning the manuscript.

Beth Goobie

About Beth Goobie

Beth Goobie spent five and a half years working in locked and open residential treatment settings for children and teens. She is also a multi-award winning author who has published books for both young adult and adult audiences. She has appeared on the American Library Association's Best Books list, been nominated for two Governor General's Awards, and won the Canadian Library Association's Young Adult Book Award. Beth studied at the University of Winnipeg and lives in Saskatoon, Saskatchewan.

Also by Beth Goobie

Novels for Young People
Born Ugly
Hello Groin
Fixed
Flux
Sticks and Stones
The Lottery
Before Wings
The Dream Where the Losers Go
Something Girl
The Colours of Carol Molev
The Good, the Bad, and the Suicidal
I'm Not Convinced
Kicked Out
Who Owns Kelly Paddick
Hit and Run
Mission Impossible
Group Homes from Outer Space

Poetry
Scars Of Light
The Girls Who Dream Me

Adult Novels
The Only-Good Heart
Could I Have My Body Back Now, Please?